Adeline's Porcupine

Bobby Strickland

Illustrated by Kathryn Rathke

BakerBooks
Grand Rapids, Michigan

For Don, who allowed me to love my inner porcupine.
—*Bobby*

To my sister Liz, and the drawings of our youth.
—*Kathryn*

Published by Baker Books
a division of Baker Book House Company
P.O. Box 6287, Grand Rapids, MI 49516-6287
www.bakerbooks.com

Printed in the United States of America

Published in association with the literary agency of Ann Spangler and Company, 1420 Pontiac Road Southeast, Grand Rapids, Michigan 49506.

Library of Congress Cataloging-in-Publication Data
Strickland, Bobby, 1960–
    Adeline's porcupine / Bobby Strickland ; illustrated by Kathryn Rathke.
        p.   cm.
    Summary: Young Adeline's pet porcupine feels sad because she is not as beautiful as the arrogant city pets, but her inner beauty and compassion help the other pets discover her true worth.
    ISBN 0-8010-4507-X (cloth)
    [1. Beauty, Personal—Fiction. 2. Porcupines—Fiction. 3. Self-esteem—Fiction. 4. Stories in rhyme.] I. Rathke, Kathryn, ill. II. title
PZ8.3.S8555Ag 2004
[E]—dc22   2003024255

Bobby Strickland, a reluctant adult, is a professional Christian counselor in the Atlanta, Georgia, area. He began writing the *Adeline* stories as a gift for a friend who had just given birth to her first daughter. The whimsical series of poems were turned into books at the urging of friends and colleagues.

Kathryn Rathke is a professional illustrator and set designer in Seattle, Washington. Her work appears in numerous periodicals, including the *Stranger*, the *Washington Post*, *New York Press*, and the *Progressive*. She has also designed scenery for several critically acclaimed theatrical productions.

The illustrations in this book were rendered in pen and ink.
The text type is set in Utopia.
The display type is set in Jelly Bean.

Art direction by Paula Gibson
Design by Brian Brunsting

In Zeeland, they say, at the edge of the wood,

where Adeline Addison's little house stood,

a family of porcupines made their abode

in an old hollow tree by the side of the road.

Their little tree home was too small for the bunch,

and with seventeen children, they lived in a crunch.

To make matters worse, Mrs. Porcupine knew

she would soon have a baby to add to her crew.

At last the day came when her baby was born,

a sweet little daughter but small and forlorn.

Her thin little body was covered with quills

to protect her from danger and keep her from chills.

"I'm afraid we can't keep you," the sad mother cried

as she wrapped up her baby and took her outside.

"We have nothing to feed you. The cupboards are bare.

I must find you a home where you'll have proper care."

So within a small basket her poor baby lay,

to be left on sweet Adeline's doorstep that day.

Then the sad mother hid in the bushes and prayed
until Adeline found where the orphan was laid.

"A present!" said Adeline. "When did this come?"
And she looked for a note to see who it was from.

Then she heard a small whimper and saw a pink snout.

"It's a baby," she cried, "and it wants to get out!

It's a porcupine baby; she's hungry and wet.

Come inside, little one. I will make you my pet."

Now the porcupine
wasn't a beautiful sight.
She was prickly and awkward
and somewhat a fright.

But because she was kind,
with a heart like pure gold,
her beauty inside
was a joy to behold.

So Adeline named
her pet porcupine Grace
for the love and compassion
she saw on her face.

And when Grace became sad because she wasn't pretty,

it was Adeline's words that could soothe her self-pity:

"How you look, little one, cannot measure your worth.

In your heart you're the loveliest creature on earth."

Pretty soon Grace's quills were in need of a trim.

It was time for a bath.

She looked rather grim.

So Adeline took her to Pretty Pet Grooming

for expert attention (so they were assuming).

Yet as soon as they got there the outing was doomed.

All the upper-class pets had come in to be groomed.

There were arrogant Afghans and stuck-up Siamese

and fluffy red chow chows who spoke in Chinese,

parrots and ferrets and silver-white Persians, potbellied pigs

in all possible versions!

And there on her throne at the end of the hall
sat Penelope Poodle, the queen of them all.

Penelope Poodle was snooty and proud.
Her soft, curly coat
was as white as a cloud.

She was pampered and privileged
and well pedigreed
but remarkably evil
in word and in deed.

Her family tree could be traced back to France
(and she'd fake a French accent if given the chance).
Her collar of diamonds and matching barrette
had belonged (so she said) to Marie Antoinette.

"Tomorrow's the pet show,"
Penelope scoffed,
"and we're here to be beautified,
fluffed up, and coiffed!

As for you, porcupine,
well, you might as well go.
Only beautiful pets
can compete in this show!"

All the beautiful pets believed "Poodle knows best,"

so what was good for Penelope went for the rest.

And since Princess Penelope hated poor Grace,

all the others were mean to the porcupine's face.

Grace wanted to cry, and her face grew bright red.

Then she remembered what beautiful Adeline said:

"How you look, little one,

cannot measure your worth.

In your heart you're the loveliest

creature on earth."

"Come along, little Grace!" announced sweet Adeline.

"We will enter this show, and your beauty will shine!"

So Adeline took
little Grace to her room
and sprinkled her pet
with her sweetest perfume.

Then she gave her a couple
of vitamin pills
and tied purple ribbons
on each of her quills.

"Oh, how precious!" said Adeline, looking at Grace,
and the tiniest smile lit the porcupine's face.
"Now you're ready to show them how special you are,
but remember, you'll always be my little star."

As Grace entered the ballroom, Penelope frowned.

There was no way she'd see that young porcupine crowned.

"Well, look at the pin cushion!" sneered the French dog.

"I've seen prettier things living under a log!"

"Now, Miss Poodle,"

protested a small Persian cat,

"just for once could you show

more compassion than that?"

"Oh, be quiet, you hair ball," Penelope quipped.

"You'll be out in the alley if you don't keep it zipped!

And the rest of you creatures better fall into line.

We'll have nothing to do with this sad porcupine!"

So they laughed

and they ridiculed Grace with their jeers,

and her shoe-button eyes filled with porcupine tears.

"Little Grace," whispered Adeline, "keep up your chin!

It's a shame they can't see all your beauty within."

Then she scooped up the porcupine into her purse

and carried her home, reciting this verse:

"How you look, little one, cannot measure your worth.

In your heart you're the loveliest creature on earth."

Little Grace thought all night on what Adeline said.

It was true, she was beautiful inside her head!

Though the city pets' teasing was spiteful and heartless,

Grace wanted to show her compassion regardless.

But in order to let her true beauty shine fully,

she would have to revisit that snooty French bully.

So Grace climbed again into Adeline's purse

(though she had to admit she was nervous at first).

But Adeline's verse gave her courage to go,

and they left for Penelope's hilltop chateau.

When Penelope heard a small knock at the gate,

she lifted her sunglasses, looking irate.

"It's that porcupine, Grace. What is she doing here?

Have I not made my wishes perfectly clear?"

"Miss Poodle," said Grace,

"I don't mean to offend.

I just wanted to ask you . . .

May I be your friend?"

But Penelope snapped,

"Do you think I'm a fool?"

Then her diamond tiara

fell into the pool.

"My prize!" yelped the dog,

and before she could think

she jumped into the water

but started to sink!

"I forgot! I can't swim!

I just wanted my crown!

But I can't even dog-paddle!

Don't let me drown!"

Well, the other posh pets

only stood at the rim,

because none of them, either,

had learned how to swim.

"I can save her!" cried Grace.

"Put aside all your doubts.

I was taught how to swim back in Porcupine Scouts."

With the speed of a dolphin and skill like an otter,

little Grace used her quills to cut into the water.

Compassion and mercy compelled her to pray
as she swam to the depths where Penelope lay:

"Now I ask you, dear God, give me strength from above
as I show this poor poodle the power of love."

Then she grabbed the limp dog by the back of her neck

and courageously dragged her out onto the deck.

Her heart had no pulse

and her lungs no inflation.

So Grace filled her lungs with her porcupine breath

and saved the poor dog from the clutches of death!

Penelope sputtered and splattered and opened her eyes.

Then she smiled very sweetly, to Grace's surprise.

"Oh, thank you, dear Grace!" said the wet poodle queen.

"What beauty's within you that I've never seen!

From now on you and I will be closest of friends!"

And they hugged and they cried and they made their amends.

So Grace became loved by the pets of the town,

and they joyously gave her Penelope's crown.

The *Zeeland Gazette* came to cover the story
of Adeline's porcupine risen to glory,
and on the front page was Penelope's face,
with a headline atop that read,

DOG SAVED BY GRACE.

So Adeline patted her porcupine's head

and whispered to Grace as she tucked her in bed,

"How you look, little one, cannot measure your worth.

In your heart you're the loveliest creature on earth.

You know true lovingkindness will set you apart.

Others look on the outside, but God sees the heart."